Lincoln Center

Alice in
Wonderland
statue,
Central
Park

Chinatown

Grand Central Station

ON THE LOOSE IN NEW YORK CITY

Dear Animal Detectives,

The animals included in this book are ones I thought you would recognize and have fun finding (at least in these pages) on the streets of New York City. Many of them can be found at the Central Park Zoo. Because the zoo is constantly moving animals to other zoos around the country and bringing in new animals from countries around the globe, it's always exciting to find out what animals the zoo has at any given time. The Central Park Zoo currently houses more than 130 species, including many that are rare or endangered. For more information, visit https://centralparkzoo.com. Or, better yet, visit the zoo in person.

P.S. In real life the zoo does an excellent job making sure its animals are very happy at home and don't go wandering off!

ON THE LOOSE
IN NEW YORK CITY

A Find-the-Animals Book

Written and Illustrated
by Sage Stossel

Commonwealth Editions
Carlisle, Massachusetts

FOR
MIKE AND KIERAN

ISBN 978-1-938700-16-3

Series design by John Barnett/4 Eyes Design

Commonwealth Editions is an imprint of Applewood Books, Inc.
Carlisle, Massachusetts 01741
Visit us on the web at www.commonwealtheditions.com

Visit Sage Stossel on the web at www.sagestossel.com

Printed in China

10 9 8 7 6 5 4 3 2 1

On Manhattan Island,
inside Central Park,
lies a quaint little zoo
that closes at dark.

One morning the keeper
discovered a note:
"We've gone for a walk,"
the animals wrote.

"Oh, dear!" said the keeper.
"What am I to do?
My critters have left me
alone at the zoo!"

central park zoo

The cages, indeed, were all empty that day,
for the creatures, it seemed, had meandered away.

2 penguins, 2 monkeys, 1 lizard, 1 bat, 3 bears, 1 pig, 1 snow leopard,
2 sea lions, 1 goat, 3 turtles, 1 peacock, 1 anteater, and 2 snakes

CAN YOU FIND

Then from down in the Village there came a news flash:
there's a sea lion here showing off his mustache!

1 sea lion, 1 snow leopard, 1 llama, 2 bears, 1 bat, 3 snakes, 2 monkeys,
1 anteater, 1 lizard, 2 penguins, 1 pig, 1 parrot, and 1 turtle

CAN YOU FIND

A complaint was next lodged by a sightseeing cruise:
"There are beasts on our boat, and they're blocking the views!"

2 bears, 1 llama, 1 snow leopard, 3 sea lions, 2 penguins, 1 snake, 1 turtle, 2 monkeys, 1 owl, 1 parrot, 1 anteater, and 1 peacock

CAN YOU FIND

A commotion then broke out on Museum Mile,
where a snow monkey stopped to see art for a while.

3 monkeys, 1 llama, 5 bears, 1 parrot, 1 snow leopard, 2 sea lions,
1 lizard, 3 snakes, 2 penguins, 1 turtle, and 1 anteater

Perplexed Times Square tourists weren't sure what to do
when a real grizzly posed with fake Winnie the Pooh.

2 bears, 1 pig, 1 snow leopard, 1 bat, 2 penguins, 1 lizard, 2 sea lions,
5 monkeys, 2 llamas, 1 anteater, 1 peacock, 1 snake, and 2 turtles

CAN YOU FIND

Said Central Park bird-watchers, "*This* can't be right!"
when an Antarctic penguin popped into their sight.

2 penguins, 2 bears, 2 snow leopards, 2 monkeys, 1 turtle, 1 anteater, 2 sea lions, 1 bat, 1 snake, 1 owl, 1 peacock, and 1 lizard

CAN YOU FIND

The traders on Wall Street were rather bemused
when a bull and a bear read the financial news.

1 bull, 1 bear, 1 turtle, 2 llamas, 1 snow leopard, 2 sea lions, 1 anteater, 1 sheep, 2 monkeys, 3 snakes, 2 bats, 2 lizards, and 2 penguins

CAN YOU FIND

Uptown in Harlem, the mood was upbeat,
though traffic was blocked by a large parakeet.

1 parakeet , 2 owls, 2 bears, 2 sea lions, 1 anteater, 1 snow leopard,
1 lizard, 1 bat, 1 llama, 1 turtle, 1 snake, 1 peacock, and 2 penguins

CAN YOU FIND

Theater-goers were duly impressed
by a talented leopard, performing with zest.

1 snow leopard, 1 peacock, 1 anteater, 1 bat, 3 monkeys, 2 sea lions, 1 snake, 1 turtle, 1 llama, 2 penguins, and 1 bear

CAN YOU FIND

In the great hall of dinosaurs, folks were surprised
that some creatures on view proved to be quite alive.

2 anteaters, 2 bears, 1 snow leopard, 1 snake, 2 sea lions, 1 peacock, 5 penguins, 2 turtles, 1 bat, 3 monkeys, and 1 owl

CAN YOU FIND

Quaint Little Italy served up fine treats
to a bevy of animals roaming its streets.

2 bears, 1 snake, 1 parrot, 2 anteaters, 1 snow leopard,
2 monkeys, 1 llama, 1 lizard, 1 penguin, 2 sea lions, and 1 bat

CAN YOU FIND

When at last night descended,
the zookeeper smiled,
as back through the gate
all his animals filed.

What a wonderful day
they appeared to have had,
but to be back at home
they seemed equally glad.

As for where they had been,
they refused to confess,
but the keeper was smart
and could probably guess.

Can you help
these animals find
their way home
to the zoo?

Also available in this series . . .

SAGE STOSSEL is a contributing editor for the *Atlantic* and a cartoonist for the *Boston Globe*, theAtlantic.com, the *Provincetown Banner* (for which she received a New England Press Association Award), and other publications. Her cartoons have been featured by the *Washington Post*, the *New York Times Week in Review*, CNN Headline News, *Best Editorial Cartoons of the Year*, and other venues. Her graphic novel *Starling* is serialized at GoComics.com. Other books by Sage Stossel in the "On the Loose" series include *On the Loose in Boston*, *On the Loose in Philadelphia*, and *On the Loose in Washington*, D.C.

More Online...

Visit OnTheLooseNYC.com for New York City pictures to print and color, ideas for things to do around the city, and more.

The Frick Museum

Model Sailboats, Central Park

The Morgan Library

The Metropolitan Museum of Art

The High Line